Ponds

Yvonne Franklin

Ponds

Publishing Credits

Editorial Director
Dona Herweck Rice

Creative Director
Lee Aucoin

Associate Editor
James Anderson

Illustration Manager
Timothy J. Bradley

Editor-in-Chief
Sharon Coan, M.S.Ed.

Publisher
Rachelle Cracchiolo, M.S.Ed.

Science Consultants
Scot Oschman, Ph.D.
David W. Schroeder, M.S.

Teacher Created Materials

5301 Oceanus Drive
Huntington Beach, CA 92649-1030
http://www.tcmpub.com
ISBN 978-1-4333-0318-0
© 2010 Teacher Created Materials, Inc.
Made in China
Nordica.032015.CA21500127

Table of Contents

A Quiet Moment

You are floating on your back in warm, cloudy water. The sun shines on you. A water strider skids by on top of the water. A frog croaks from the shore. A dragonfly zips past your nose. "Ahh!" you sigh. This is the life. There is nothing like a swim in a quiet **pond**.

Then you hear the thud of feet on the dirt road. "Look out below!" a voice yells. A giant splash washes over you. Your quiet moment is gone. Your friend has just jumped into the water. The two of you swim and play.

What Is It?

A pond is a small, quiet body of freshwater. Freshwater does not have salt in it like ocean water does.

Water Strider

A water strider is an insect with two short legs up front and four long legs on its sides. It uses its front side legs for paddles and its back side legs for steering. Its body repels, or pushes away, water. This lets the bug stand and run on top of the water! It gets its food by feeling movement on the water's surface.

There was a time when many people lived near ponds. They used ponds for the water they needed. If there was not a **natural** pond nearby, people might dig one. They would let large holes fill with water. Plants would grow there. Animals would come, too. The pond would become a part of nature.

Today, many people have other ways to get water. Homes often have pipes that bring water into the house. Many of the old ponds dried up. But natural ponds can still be found.

People may not use ponds in the ways they once did, but ponds are an important part of nature. They are each like little worlds of their own. Animals and plants of many kinds live there. They depend on each other to live. The world of a pond is a fascinating place.

If you saw a pond, you just might want to jump in to be a part of it!

Ponds do not have moving water like many other water bodies do.

They Don't Live Forever

If ponds are left alone, they will slowly fill in with dirt and dry up. But this may take hundreds of years.

What Is a Pond?

Most of the water on Earth is in oceans. Rain and melted snow run down to **sea level** in rivers and streams. Large amounts of water collect in lakes. Ponds are not really like any of these water bodies.

Ponds are small. They are about 1–4 meters (3–13 feet) deep. They are often made from rainwater or groundwater. The water collects in a pit in the ground. Ponds are shallow enough that sunlight can reach to the bottom. That does not happen in deep oceans and lakes where the bottom is often dark. Ponds may be filled with light.

Across the Pond

When people say that they are going "across the pond," they mean that they are traveling across the Atlantic Ocean. The Atlantic Ocean is certainly not a pond! People call it a pond as a way to be funny.

Light is able to reach to the bottom of ponds where the ground is muddy.

Many plants can grow in a pond when there is a lot of sunlight. They grow from shore to shore across the bottom and sides of the pond. They grow on the banks of the pond, too. The land around the pond is often a **marsh**. A marsh is low, wet land that may be covered in grasses. Insects, birds, reptiles, and **amphibians** (am-FIB-ee-uhns) make their homes in and near ponds. Some **mammals** live in and near them, too.

Some plants grow only under the water of a pond. Some reach above the surface. Some float on the surface! You may have read make-believe stories with lily pads on the water where magical frogs live. Lily pads are the floating leaves of water lily plants. Water lilies grow in many ponds.

marsh plants

emerging plants

Come and Go

Ponds may only have water in them for as few as four months a year. They may be dry or just muddy in the other months.

Each plant finds the perfect spot to live.

floating plants

submerged plants

emerging plants

marsh plants

lily pads, or leaves, from water lilies

When plants and animals die in a pond, they drop to the bottom. They **decompose**, or rot, there. The **nutrients** (NOO-tree-uhnts) from their bodies go into the earth and water. They feed new plants and animals. But this process uses up **oxygen**, too. Animals need **oxygen** to live. So, there may be fewer animals near the pond floor than close to the surface.

Water temperatures in ponds stay pretty even throughout the whole pond. The water at the surface feels a lot like the water at the bottom. The water temperature is about the same as the air temperature. A warm day means a warm pond. A cold day means a cold pond.

Most bodies of water do not freeze all the way in cold weather. But ponds do. They are so shallow that the whole thing may freeze solid.

Flatworm

A flatworm's body has a lot of surface area. This helps the flatworm to take in more oxygen. So, a flatworm can live easily in the mud at the bottom of a pond.

Pond water stays fairly calm. There are really no waves in ponds. Wind may stir the water a little, but usually the water is quite still.

frozen pond

Life in a Pond

The rich plant life makes ponds a great place for animals to live. The plants and animals are connected in an **ecosystem** (EK-oh-sis-tuhm). An ecosystem is made of plants, animals, water, land, and air. The animals and plants depend on one another. They use the land, water, and air to live.

The word *ecosystem* has two parts: *eco* and *system*. *Eco* comes from the Greek word for house. A system is a combination of parts that make a whole. Those two parts of the word *ecosystem* can help to understand what it is.

Think of a family in a house. The family (living things) needs the house and what is in it to live. The people need the food in the cupboards. They need the water in the plumbing. They need the clothes in the closets. They need the air in the rooms. Each of these things helps the family to live and thrive.

A pond is like that. Animals and plants can thrive because of the food, water, and shelter found there. A pond makes the perfect ecosystem.

swallow

great crested newt

eel

hawk

otter

water vole

dragonfly

microscopic life

In this pond ecosystem, there are many animals and plants which live together.

A pond may be small, but a huge number of animals and plants may live there. The chart on this page shows some of the animals that may be found in or near a pond.

Insects live on, in, and around ponds. Some mosquitoes (muh-SKEE-tohs) lay their eggs on the water.

Invertebrates (in-VUR-tuh-brits) such as leeches love pond life. A leech is like a thick worm. It can hide in the mud at the bottom of a pond. It sucks the blood of its **prey**.

Amphibians such as salamanders (SAL-uh-man-ders) have moist skin. They stay near and in the water. Salamanders are interesting. If they lose a limb, they can grow a new one!

Birds such as herons nest near ponds. But they wade in the water and often get food there.

Mammals such as beavers can make homes in or near ponds. Beavers build lodges out of sticks and mud. Some beaver dams are more than 800 meters (2,625 feet) long!

Pond Animals

Insects	Invertebrates	Amphibians
dragonfly	clam	frog
fire ant	crayfish	newt
mosquito	leech	salamander
water strider	shrimp	toad
Reptiles	**Birds**	**Mammals**
copperhead snake	Canada goose	beaver
garter snake	crane	muskrat
painted turtle	duck	opossum
snapping turtle	heron	raccoon

mosquito
laying eggs

beaver

leech

snapping
turtle

salamander

heron

17

Pond animals need the plants in the pond. Plants give shelter and food. Submerged plants also **aerate** (AIR-ate), or give oxygen, to the water. These plants live below the water's surface.

Floating and emerging plants make food for animals. Insects and other creatures can rest on them. Bank and marsh plants are good places for animals to hide and build shelter. They are also food for animals.

Bacteria

Bacteria (bak-TEER-ee-uh) are important parts of ponds. Bacteria are tiny. Animals feed on them. Then bacteria decompose the dead bodies of animals and plants.

bacteria as seen through a microscope

pondweed

duckweed

oxygen bubbles

St. John's wort

lotus

Pond Plants

Floating Plants	Submerged Plants	Emerging Plants	Bank and Marsh Plants
duckweed	pondweed	lotus	cattail
frogbit	hornwort	pennywort	reed
water hyacinth	monkey tail	pickerel plant	rush
water lettuce	water violet	water lily	St. John's wort

eggs

tadpole

Frog
Life Cycle

adult frog

tadpole with
front legs

A Pond's Life Cycle

Many things in nature are part of a **cycle**. A cycle is something that follows from start to finish and back again. It repeats over and over. Living things have a life cycle. They are born, grow up, have children, and die. The children become adults. This is the cycle.

The seasons are a cycle. Day and night are parts of a cycle, too.

You probably know the life cycle of many pond animals. For example, frogs begin as eggs. They become tadpoles. Then they grow legs. They lose their tails. They become adult frogs. Then they lay eggs, and the cycle starts again.

The pond itself is part of a cycle, too.

tadpole
with hind
legs

Energy Web

One of the most common cycles in nature is an energy web. Every living thing has energy. At each stage of the energy web, energy is passed from one thing to another. So, an insect may eat bacteria. A fish may eat the insect. A bird may eat the fish. A mammal may eat the bird. Then, the mammal may die. Bacteria will decompose the mammal's body. The cycle of energy goes on and on.

There is a lot of activity in a pond during the spring and summer. Insects buzz. Birds nest. Fish swim. Mammals roam. The pond is full of growing plants. The water is aerated, or rich with oxygen.

In the winter, the weather may turn very cold. In some places, it freezes. Ponds are shallow. So, all of the water may freeze. The oxygen gets used up. The life in the pond will rest, go away, or die.

When the weather warms, the pond will thaw. Wind may stir up the water. New water may flow or rain into the pond. The pond becomes aerated in this way. Plants grow again. Animals return to their pond home.

Cattails

There are about 250,000 seeds on one cattail stalk!

cattail stalks

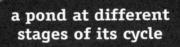

a pond at different stages of its cycle

Ponds may go through another kind of cycle as well. Ponds are **fragile**. That means they may change easily.

A healthy pond is filled with animals and plants. The healthier it becomes, the more plants and animals grow. Dead plants and animals begin to fill the bottom of the pond. Dirt and mud may fill the bottom as well. More plants grow in all the nutrients. Over time, the pond fills in. It becomes part of the marsh that is all around it. In time, the plants may die away. Water may fill the hole again. A new pond may form.

In nature, you can count on some cycles. For example, day always follows night. But you never know when a pond will form, or when it will become something else all together.

Algae

Algae (AL-jee) may grow thickly in ponds. Algae is a plant-like living thing that can create a lot of oxygen in a pond. It is red, green, or brown in color. Algae can be as tiny as one cell or as large as a giant seaweed.

algae

This pond is slowly filling in and may soon look similar to the prairie around it.

Pollution can kill a pond quickly. People should do their parts in protecting the delicate life of ponds.

At Risk

Since there is not a lot of water moving in a pond, pollution can be a big problem. Once polluted water gets in, it affects the whole pond. The pollution does not just get washed away. Bacteria and other small animals work hard to keep the pond clean and healthy. But they need oxygen to do the work. Polluted water has less oxygen.

When a pond is sick, oxygen at the bottom can go a long way toward making it healthy again. People can help by aerating the water. People can cut down on pollution, too. A little care can go a long way!

When people take care of nature, nature will take care of people, too.

Lab: Ant Farm

One of the best ways to learn about cycles in nature is to observe them. Some of nature's smallest creatures have some of the most fascinating lives! Ants, for example, are well organized and work hard all their lives. You can build an ant farm to observe how ants live. Be sure to treat the ants with respect. They are living things, after all.

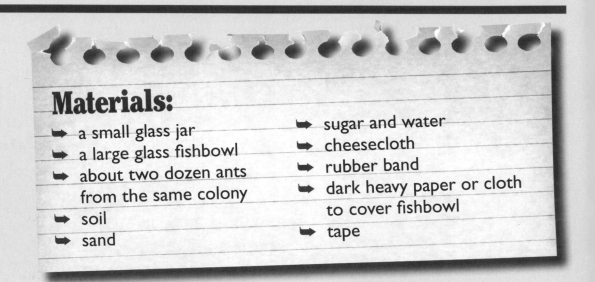

Materials:

→ a small glass jar
→ a large glass fishbowl
→ about two dozen ants from the same colony
→ soil
→ sand
→ sugar and water
→ cheesecloth
→ rubber band
→ dark heavy paper or cloth to cover fishbowl
→ tape

Procedure:

1. Carefully collect about two dozen ants from a single colony. If they are not from the same colony, they will fight.

2. Put the small glass jar upside down inside the large fishbowl.

3. Mix soil and sand so that it is loose. Pour it into the fishbowl.

4. Mix a little water and sugar together. Use the eyedropper to put several drops of the mixture in the sandy soil.

5. Add the ants to the fishbowl.

6. Cover the lid of the fishbowl with cheesecloth and a rubber band to keep the ants from getting out.

7. Wrap the dark paper or cloth around the fishbowl and tape it in place. This will make the ants think they are in the dark underground.

8. Store the fishbowl at room temperature someplace quiet. Each day, add some drops of water to the soil. Each week, add some drops of sugar water. (Just drop the water or sugar water on the surface this time.)

9. Take off the dark covering each day to observe what the ants are doing. They will begin to build tunnels and make rooms in just a few days. Be sure to cover them up again soon so that you do not disturb them.

10. Write what you see. What do you notice about ants?

Glossary

aerate—to add oxygen to

amphibian—a cold-blooded vertebrate that usually lives in or near the water

cycle—a periodically repeated sequence of events

decompose—to break down organisms

ecosystem—a geographical area where plants, animals, land, and weather all interact together

fragile—easily damaged

invertebrate—an animal without a backbone

mammal—a warm-blooded animal with fur or hair that gives birth to live young

marsh—a wet area of land that commonly grows grasses and other such plants

natural—part of nature

nutrients—nutrition from food

oxygen—the gas that makes up a large part of Earth's atmosphere and that animals breathe to live

pond—a small, fresh body of water

prey—an animal that is hunted by another animal for food

sea level—the water level of the oceans of the world

submerged—under the water

Index

Scientists Then and Now

John Muir
(1838–1914)

John Muir was born in Scotland. He always loved nature. As a young man, John began attending "the university of the wilderness." He learned by seeing things for himself. He traveled to Yosemite Valley in California to explore nature there. He wanted to protect the valley for the future. So, he helped make it a national park. He also helped form the Sierra Club. It is a group devoted to protecting nature.

Jessica L. Deichmann
(1980–)

Jessica Deichmann is an ecologist. She studies nature and the environment. She especially loves to learn about frogs, lizards, and snakes. She travels a lot to see these creatures in their own environments. She also teaches people how to help protect the animals. Jessica does everything she can to protect wildlife now and for the future.